Knifepoint

Knifepoint

Alex Van Tol

orca soundings

ORCA BOOK PUBLISHERS

Library and Archives Canada Cataloguing in Publication

Van Tol, Alex
Knifepoint / written by Alex Van Tol.
(Orca soundings)

Issued also in an electronic format.
ISBN 978-1-55469-306-1 (bound).--ISBN 978-1-55469-305-4 (pbk.)

I. Title. II. Series: Orca soundings
PS8643.A63K53 2010   JC813'.6   C2010-903604-2

First published in the United States, 2010
Library of Congress Control Number: 2010929071

Summary: Jill is enduring a brutal summer job on a mountain ranch,
guiding wannabe-cowboys on trail rides. On a solo ride with a handsome
stranger she ends up in a fight for her life with no one to help her.

Mixed Sources
Cert no. SW-COC-001271
© 1996 FSC
FSC

*Orca Book Publishers is dedicated to preserving the environment and has printed this
book on paper certified by the Forest Stewardship Council.*

Orca Book Publishers gratefully acknowledges the support for its publishing
programs provided by the following agencies: the Government of Canada
through the Canada Book Fund and the Canada Council for the Arts,
and the Province of British Columbia through the BC Arts Council
and the Book Publishing Tax Credit.

Cover design by Teresa Bubela
Cover photography by Getty Images

ORCA BOOK PUBLISHERS
PO Box 5626, Stn. B
VICTORIA, BC Canada
V8R 6S4

ORCA BOOK PUBLISHERS
PO Box 468
CUSTER, WA USA
98240-0468

www.orcabook.com
Printed and bound in Canada.

13 12 11 10 • 4 3 2 1

For Barb and Jan,
who reminded me I was a writer.

Chapter One

Voices, sudden and loud, jolt me out of my dream. Confused, I try to sit up. But I can't. It feels like I've been tied to the bed with a million tiny threads. I force one eye open. Turn my head. The clock radio says *6:44*. The voices keep shouting. They're coming from the radio. The same radio I've woken up to for the past thirty-five days, at the same ungodly hour.

Except every morning it gets harder.

I raise my head and look at the wooden walls. A million tiny daggers shoot through my skull. Ugh. I prop myself on one elbow and hit *Snooze*. The daggers turn into hammers and spread out across my body. About a thousand go to work on the soles of my feet. I swing my feet out of bed, careful not to touch them to the floor. I can't face that agony yet. Yawning, I reach for some socks. I've *got* to start going to bed earlier. I can't keep functioning on five hours of sleep a night. Not when my job beats the crap out of me every day.

The metal bedframe squeaks as I heave myself up. Owww, ow. I could die right about now. If a serial killer poked his head into my room and offered to stab me at this exact moment,

I'd tell him to go right ahead. I wonder if it's normal for my feet to hurt this much.

Well, yeah, maybe. When you spend fourteen hours working and then another five dancing nonstop. But it's so fun!

I glance at the clock again. *6:53.* I shove my screaming feet into my cowboy boots. I look at them. They're filthy, caked in horseshit after the July rains. I'm not supposed to wear them inside the bunkhouse, but whatever. I can't scrub the crap off either. I've tried. It's all over the bottom of my chaps too. That's a bummer. I spent a lot to have those custom made. That was back when I thought I'd be making $12.50 an hour.

Back before I found out that what James really meant was $1250 *a month.*

Slave labor, that's what it is. Kristi and I calculated it a few weeks ago— a couple of days before she ditched the ranch to go find a decent-paying job in

3

the city. Turns out I make about $4.46 an hour. It's *hard* work, too, being a wrangler: chucking hay bales, hefting saddles, dragging buckets of grain, pushing and pulling around 1500-pound animals all day long.

Thinking of the horses gets me moving. The first barn shift starts at seven, and being late sucks. If you start your morning late, you spend all day playing catch-up.

I leave the rest of the bunkhouse sleeping, closing the door softly behind me.

The cold morning air stings my throat as I hobble across the grass to the main lodge. My feet are killing me. Heavy dew darkens my boots. God, it feels like winter's coming already. I shiver, wishing I'd dug around to find my gloves.

I push open the screen door leading to the kitchen. Steve, the morning cook, hands me a muffin on my way through. He's nice enough but looks like he just escaped maximum-security prison. Who knows, maybe he did. They're not particularly strict with their hiring practices around here. Steve has so many tattoos it's hard to see any un-inked flesh on his arms. I like him though. He feeds me for free. The other cooks make you punch a meal card if you want so much as a package of saltines.

"You look like shit, Jill," he says pleasantly.

"Kiss my chaps, kitchen boy," I snarl over my shoulder.

Steve laughs, then growls at me. "With pleasure."

Pit stop at the coffee machine. Then straight out to the barn. Hopefully there won't be a nine o'clock ride. If there isn't, I'll be able to come back into the restaurant and eat a proper breakfast after I get the horses saddled.

No one's at the barn when I get there. I figured as much. Carrie and Laura downed a whole lot of beer last night. It's not the first time they haven't shown up for their shift. And I'm certain it won't be the last either. They get away with murder, those two. Jerks. If *I* ever overslept and missed the start of my shift, I'd sure as hell hear about it. But they're the queen bees, so I keep my head down and my mouth shut.

Whiskey snorts in recognition when she sees me. I give her a quick brush, pitch a blanket and saddle onto her back and sling a bridle over her soft face.

Where's Kim? I'd almost be glad to see her grumpy butt marching around the corral this morning, swearing at random horses and kicking any that looked at her the wrong way. She's a total cow. But I gotta say, she gets stuff done around the barn. If she was here, she'd have dragged Carrie and Laura out of bed by their long sexy hair. She's the only one who'd dare.

Now I remember. It's Kim's day off. Damn. No Kim, no Carrie, no Laura. No one else on the schedule. I'll have to round up the horses on my own.

All sixty of them.

I swallow my butterflies and swing up onto Whiskey's back. I turn her head toward the night pasture.

I have no idea whether I'll be able to gather up five dozen horses and herd them in one tidy bunch toward the barn. I'm not a born-and-raised cowhand by any stretch. As far as I know, nobody has ever rounded up on their own. Lucky me. But what else can I do? I can't wait until one of the beautiful drunkards staggers in for her shift. That could be hours. By then there'll be guests lined up along the corral fences, waiting for their trail rides.

I've got to do it.

When we get there, Whiskey and I run a quick perimeter check around the night pasture. I crack the whip and get them all moving toward the gate.

I wait until every horse is crammed up against the fence, noses, necks and bums all crowded together in a warm shifting mass. Whiskey and I wedge our way along the fence to the gate. I hold my breath and flip the latch off the gatepost. The gate groans open, powered by a dozen hungry horses.

I crack the whip. "Hyaaaaagh! *Let's go, boys!*"

Startled, the horses bolt straight out of the gate and pound along the road leading to the barn.

Right on. *Go, Jill!* I give Whiskey a kick and we lurch away, chasing the heels of the horses at the back. "Hyaaagh!" Over and over I shout and crack the whip. The horses thunder along the road, kicking up dust in the morning sunlight. They hammer into the main corral and spread out along the fences, content to be hemmed in again. I close the corral gate behind them and slide to the ground, surprised that my shaking knees hold me up.

"Nice work," says an appreciative voice. I spin around. A guy I don't recognize is leaning against the fence. He's maybe in his mid-twenties. Dark hair. Red shirt. He flashes a grin at me. *Oh.* And he's gorgeous. Was he watching that whole time? I feel myself flush. Stupid.

"Thanks." I can't think of anything else to say, so I tie Whiskey to a fence-post and loosen her saddle. I jerk a halter off a peg and walk out into the corral. I slide it over Ace's head and lead him into the barn. I grab another halter.

"I'm Darren Parker. From Bar G," he says. His voice is friendly. I know that ranch. It's just up the valley, about twenty minutes away. "You guys do adventure rides?"

I swallow. An adventure ride? Yeah, we do them. But I sure hope that's not what he's after. A trail ride is one thing. The horses just line up and follow each other's butts through the forest for a couple of hours. But adventure rides? Crashing through rivers, pelting down hills and racing through meadows? I hate taking out adventure rides.

Don't get me wrong. I love running my horse fast and taking crazy chances. But I don't like being responsible for other people during a fast, risky ride. I don't have the same kind of horse background that the other wranglers have.

Nope, adventure rides aren't my thing. It's hard enough for me to hang on to my own damn horse, let alone look after someone else's.

But I don't say any of this. Maybe this guy will be able to handle himself. Being a wrangler and all.

"Rides start at nine o'clock." I glance at him. "You might as well go in and have breakfast while you wait."

With that, I turn back to the work of catching horses. And I hope to hell that he can't hear my heart as it tries to pound its way through my chest.

Chapter Two

I work like a fiend. By a quarter to nine I've got ten horses fed, brushed and saddled. I stand in the middle of the barn, wiping my brow with my sleeve. It's going to be a hot day.

The horses rustle and munch their way through the hay I've forked up into their feed baskets. I'm even more tired than I was when I first woke up.

My throat is dry and my stomach is rumbling. But I don't have time to eat. Not yet, anyway.

I unscrew the cap on my water bottle and take a long drink. I cast a quick glance toward the bunkhouse, hoping that Carrie and Laura are on their way over. Please, please let someone show up before this adventure ride goes out. As cute as Mr. Bar G is, I still don't feel like racing across ridgetops with him.

God, I feel like such a chicken sometimes. I hate it. I wish I could be as comfortable and brave on a horse as Carrie is. She's just totally dialed in to what it means to ride. She and her horse are, like, *one*. Thinking and acting in tandem. I can't help but feel envious. I'm still trying to figure out how to run with my reins in one hand instead of grabbing onto the saddle horn to keep from bouncing off. It's a wonder James hired me at all.

But I know why he did. It was obvious when we met last April that there was some pretty good chemistry between us. He put me up on a horse and asked me to ride around in a circle. Walk, trot, canter. When I didn't fall off, I guess he figured I was good enough for the job.

James's parents own the ranch. And he hired all the summer barn staff. Not surprisingly, we're all girls around the same age. Long hair. Long legs. James likes his ladies. I could tell he liked looking at me. Not that I minded. He has the hugest, bluest eyes I've ever seen. And the way he wears his black hat pulled low on his brow... he's all dark and broodingly handsome. I still get a shiver when I think of him. Even now that things aren't so good between us.

James got pretty huffy a few weeks back when he found out I have a boyfriend back in the city. Tyler.

But it's pretty casual between Ty and me. Actually, it's kind of on hold. I'm the one who decided to leave town for the summer. But whatever. When James found out, he got really mad. It was like he thought I'd tricked him by not telling him about Tyler right away. He gave me the silent treatment for, like, a week. I thought that was pretty lame, especially for a guy who's nineteen.

Eventually he came out of his funk and we started talking again. But he stopped spending time with me. And he stopped taking rides out with me. He started hanging around with Carrie and Laura instead.

Yeah, and we all know how much work Carrie and Laura do around the ranch.

That was a couple of weeks ago. Nowadays, it's pretty much me and a couple of other wranglers—Martin and Roxanne—who take out all the rides.

James stays back at the barn to flirt with Laura and Carrie. I guess he figures the ranch is kind of his, which gives him permission to be lazy and duck responsibility. And that pisses me right off.

Yesterday, James and I finally had a blowout. It was bound to happen. I had just come back from a half-day ride. I was hot. Thirsty. My knees hurt after sitting astride a horse's barrel for three hours. I hadn't eaten since 6:45 that morning, and I was starving.

I figured I'd be able to go in and have lunch before taking another ride out. But when I arrived at the barn, four guests were leaning against the corral fence, waiting to go out on a two-hour ride. Groan.

Roxanne and Martin were on their days off, so they weren't around. Carrie, Laura and James were in the back corral, just out of sight. I could hear them goofing around and cracking the whip. Ignoring the customers.

I dismounted and started helping my guests get off their horses. One guy gave me five bucks, which was cool. I took my time removing the horses' bridles and loosening their saddles. I made a big deal of looking busy. I hoped that James and the others would start to get the waiting group ready. When they kept screwing around, I finally went over to the corral.

"Hey," I said. Laura and Carrie smiled at me. Pretty smiles. All crystal and sharp edges.

"How was your ride?" Laura asked sweetly.

"Nice," I said. "I'm hungry now though. I'm going in for lunch."

"Yeah," said Carrie. "We're going to go eat too, as soon as we give Pepper a bath. We're braiding his mane and tail for the parade tomorrow." She pointed toward the dark-coated Clydesdale.

"Yeah," agreed Laura. She eyed the people standing along the corral fence. "Guess we should get started, huh, Carrie?"

Carrie sighed delicately. She handed the whip to James. "Sure. Let's go. See you guys later." And they were gone.

Slouching in disappointment, James hung the whip on a hook. I could almost see the black thundercloud forming over his head as he walked toward the tack room. I followed, starting to feel my own anger simmering. Why the hell was he going inside when he could clearly see people waiting? It was his turn to take a ride out.

"The string horses aren't in the tack room," I said coolly. "They're out in the corral. Where the next ride's waiting."

James spun around and faced me. "*Pardon*?" Acid dripped from his voice.

I was suddenly tired of his stupid games. Tired of tiptoeing around his dark moods. I pushed past him and stepped inside the tack room. "This is *your* ride," I said, nodding my head toward the corral. "I've just come off a half-day, James. And I opened this morning. I'm going in to have lunch."

And just like that, James flipped. Fuh-lipped. With two quick steps, he was in my face. His eyes blazed and his lips tightened as they turned down. He looked ugly.

I took a step backward.

"You don't tell me what to do," he snarled through gritted teeth. His breath stank of cigarettes and coffee. His voice rose. "This is *my* ranch. You work for *me*."

I squashed the urge to point out that, in fact, it wasn't his ranch. At least, not yet. But he was so worked up I was afraid that he'd clock me if I opened my mouth in argument.

James pointed outside, through the open door. I'm certain the people standing along the corral fence heard his every word. His eyes narrowed. "That's *your* ride. *You're* going to take those people out." He jabbed his finger against my breastbone as he spat the words. *"You don't tell me what to do."*

I stared at him. *Was he serious?* My mind reeled as I tried to figure out how a person could go from nasty to downright demonic in fewer than ten seconds.

James stared right back, challenging me. When I didn't move, he gave me a sour little smile.

My mind scrambled to form cohesive thoughts. The blood boiled as it rushed to my head. My lower jaw tightened. I was so angry I wanted to cry. But I ground my teeth together and bit the tears back. Crying was the last thing I'd let James see me do. I cleared my throat. Waited until I could trust my voice to be steady.

"Fine," I said. My voice shook anyway, and I hated myself for it. "I'll take this ride out. Not because you told me to, but because there are good people out there who are waiting to explore the wild Rocky Mountains on horseback. That's what they pay money to do here, at *your* ranch, James."

I turned on my heel and stormed out of the tack room.

Outside on the steps, I stopped to swipe my arm across my eyes.

Then I rounded the corner to greet my guests.

Chapter Three

Thinking about yesterday's fight with James makes my pulse quicken. I'm still so angry with him. I'm angry with myself for backing down too. I'm sure, when he finally catches up with me, he'll have a lot to say. I might even lose my job. But I guess I'm okay with that. At this point, I think I'd be fine with moving back to the city and actually making some money. I've had my nature fix. Maybe I'll start looking on Craigslist tonight. See what's out there.

Immersed in my thoughts, I don't notice Darren's return. "Ready for that adventure ride?" He's leaning on the corral fence again. Smiling at me.

My stomach does a slow dip 'n' dive, settling low within my body. I close my eyes in a final pointless prayer that one of the other wranglers will magically appear—maybe even the ranch heir himself? But no one comes. It's all up to me. This is my day to show my *cojones*, it seems. I sigh inwardly.

I work up a friendly smile and turn to Darren. This might be my last day here. Might as well make it an adventure.

"You bet," I say. "I am *so* ready."

His grin widens, and my stomach tilts sideways a bit. Oh, is he ever nice to look at. I guess this might work out to be kind of fun after all. Maybe. As long as

I can manage to stay on top of Whiskey. *Can you hold your Whiskey?* my brain bleats, and I utter a thin little laugh.

I take a few steps toward him with my hand outstretched. "I'm Jill," I offer.

His hand, warm and strong, takes mine. "Pleased to meet you, Jill," he says.

The second he touches me, I blush from my toes to the roots of my hair. I want to drop through the ground. Is anybody else witnessing my complete and utter loserdom? My eyes dart around. All is still. The flag ripples high on the pole, but otherwise there's no movement anywhere that I can see. The ranch is still dozing.

I look back at Darren. His eyes take me in, roving over my body. Not in a sicko way. Just enough to make me feel suddenly shy. I drop his hand and wipe my sweaty palm on my jeans. He smiles warmly again.

I try to get a grip on my fluttering insides. What's my deal today? This guy makes me feel like I've never flirted before in my life.

Taking a deep breath, I size Mr. Bar G up. Darren. I scan his long, lean body with the same degree of interest that he gave to mine moments ago. I decide to pair him with Springsteen, who's big and fast. And sure-footed. The last thing I need is a dude horse that loses track of its hooves on rough ground.

I slip a bridle over Springsteen's head and he takes the bit willingly. Loves to run, the hairy bugger. I tighten his saddle and stroke his neck a bit, inhaling his gorgeous hay-dirt-and-poo smell. I hand the reins to Darren.

"This is Springsteen," I say. "Climb on up. I'm going to grab my saddlebags from inside, and then we'll get moving." I head into the barn.

My eyes take a moment to adjust to the dimness inside. I fumble around in my saddlebags, feeling for my sunscreen, lip balm and water bottle. All there. Good. I take my phone out of my chest pocket and slip it into one of the soft leather bags.

I search around on the desk for a pen so I can write a note for the other wranglers to let them know what time I left. No pen. What a surprise. I find a pencil, but its lead is broken. I toss it. Whatever. I'll be back in a couple of hours. Those lazy hungover asses will probably still be asleep by the time I get back.

My coffee has gone cold, but I take one last sip and set the mug down on the desk. I'm as ready for this as I'll ever be.

I step into the corral and slip the saddlebags up behind Whiskey's saddle. I tie the leather straps to secure it, then swing up onto her back. Okay, *swing* is a bit poetic. There's nothing graceful about mounting a horse, I'm afraid. Not for me, at least. It's just a grab-and-scramble kind of thing. Once I'm up, though, I'm good to go.

I decide to skip the usual safety and skills talk. This guy's a wrangler. He looks like he knows his stuff. Doing a bit of comparison shopping at another ranch is what I figure. Seeing what kind of value we offer our guests. Taking that information back to Bar G.

Fair enough.

I decide right then and there to show him a good time.

I ease the main corral gate open, careful to close it behind me so the other horses can't get out. You only make that mistake once. It's still pretty quiet around here. I spot a couple of guests drifting back to their cabin from brunch in the main lodge. Not much else is moving. Must've been a heavy night of partying for the ranch staff.

I catch a glimpse of Jeremy through the restaurant window. He's wearing his white shirt and black tie, perfectly turned out for his shift despite probably still being hammered. We practically had to pour his ass into the car last night when we left the Ram and Raven. He waves as we pass the window, then turns his attention back to his customers. My head gives a tiny throb of sympathy for how the poor guy must be suffering. At least I was the DD last night. If I'd been drinking too, there's no way Darren would've gotten his adventure ride this morning.

Ah, yes. An adventure ride. That's what this guy's paying for, after all. So be it then. I step it up a notch, booting Whiskey into a brisk trot. We ease into a slow canter, leaving the ranch behind and entering the provincial park that borders it. Hundreds of acres of trails, river and mountains await our exploration. Never mind that the wranglers usually stick to

the same four or five well-worn trails—
it's the thought of all that unexplored
territory that makes me feel so free.
I guess I'll miss this part of the job.

We're pretty far from the ranch when
it hits me: Darren never gave me a
ticket stub for his ride. I have no way of
knowing whether he signed the waiver
form. The one that says you might die
from tripping, falling, drowning, being
eaten by a bear, burning in a forest
fire, plunging off a cliff or otherwise
meeting your untimely end in a horse's
company, so sign here on the dotted
line. In fact, I don't know if he even
paid for this ride.

Damn. That's a pretty big oversight.
I start to turn around in my saddle to
ask Darren whether he did, in fact, sign
the waiver in the main office. Maybe he
just forgot to give me his stub.

But in the next moment an evil little
thought starts to curl around the edges

of my mind. So what if he didn't sign it? He knows how to ride. I highly doubt he'll break his neck and sue. I'm probably going to get my butt fired as soon as I see James anyway. And even if I don't, I think I'm moving on, so...wouldn't it be fun for me to just... take this mystery cowboy out on a free ride? It'll be my last little *screw you* to James.

I'm so chuffed by my naughty plan that I turn around and flash Darren a full-on grin. Surprised, he grins back. Ooh, those butterflies again. With a whoop and a kick, I spur Whiskey into a hard gallop. We fly through the forest, laughing, as the morning sunshine streams through the pines.

Chapter Four

Okay, *I* fly through the forest, laughing in the sunshine. It takes a moment for me to realize I don't hear Springsteen's footfalls behind me anymore. When did I lose Darren? I slow Whiskey to a walk, and then I stop. I turn around in the saddle to look behind us. There's Darren— waaaaaay far back at the trail junction.

Jesus, is he getting back *on* his horse? When—and how—did he come off?

I pull a U-turn and canter back. Springsteen stands patiently, waiting for his rider to get it together and climb back on.

"You okay?" I ask.

He laughs nervously. "A little dusty. But I'm all right."

I slide off Whiskey and hold Springsteen while Darren climbs back on. "You're, uh…You're not a wrangler, are you, Darren Parker?"

Darren shakes his head. I expect to find embarrassment in his face, but he's got that cheerful smile pasted on. "Nope," he grins. "I'm a bartender."

I nod. I feel a bit relieved that I don't have to endure two hours of fearful risk-taking in the saddle. But part of me is disappointed all the same.

"So we'll, uh, maybe we'll take it a little bit slower?" I ask. "I mean, we'll still go on an adventure ride, just…just not a really fast one."

He grins. "Sure. A slow adventure ride sounds great."

Suddenly I have a brilliant idea. "Maybe I'll take you to the old mill site," I say. "It's totally hidden away up on a mountainside." I haven't been there in years.

"That sounds *perfect*," he says. I can tell by his face that he likes the idea. We ride side by side for a while, hemmed in by trees on one side and the river on the other. He tells me that he's from down east, here for his last "fun" summer job before he finishes his MBA in January. That he's wanted to see the Rockies his whole life, and now he's finally here. For his adventure.

I wave to a group of white-water rafters drifting by.

"Who are they?" Darren asks.

"Local rafting outfit," I answer.

"I worked for them as a river guide last summer. The Sawtooth is a popular river for white-water kayakers and rafters. Lots of good rapids." The rafters drift around a bend and out of sight. "You should try it sometime," I say. "It goes with your whole adventure theme."

"Mmm, nah," he says. "I'm not much of a swimmer. Why'd you quit rafting?"

I shrug. "It wasn't as fun as it looked. Heavy rafts, dumb tourists who don't listen. Lots of hard work."

"But you work hard at the ranch, don't you?" he asks. "I watched you bringing in the horses this morning. Didn't look like a cakewalk to me."

I laugh. "Yeah, but at least I'm an okay rider," I say. "I sucked at steering a thousand-pound raft through a white-water pinball machine."

This makes him laugh. We turn off the main trail and onto a side path.

We're headed toward the old mill.

Chapter Five

There's nobody around as we meander through a residential camp at the base of Mount Whiteridge. That's because it's Saturday afternoon. Transition day. One tired group of campers has returned home, and the next won't arrive until tomorrow. As we walk, I tell Darren about my memories of being a camper here. Living in a teepee. Canoe trips.

Midnight kitchen raids. Getting lost in the dark. Falling in love.

I keep an eye out for the wooden arrow that points the way up the hillside, toward the mill site. I remember my first visit. Our counselor took our group when I was about twelve. We spent a long time looking at the remnants of the millkeeper's home up on the mountainside. It was eerie. Almost like his spirit was still up there somewhere. Watching.

Before long I spot the faded sign. I turn Whiskey's head uphill. As I lead Darren up to the site, I wonder how much has changed in the years since I last visited. Is the old cabin still standing? Has the rusted car become overgrown by bushes?

A few minutes later, we arrive. The wooden wreckage spreads out around us. Half an acre of thin boards are piled in a huge heap, like a giant spilled a big box of matches. They're a lonely reminder of an old-timer's attempt to make a living. I always wonder why he picked a mountainside to set up the mill.

Small saplings have started to grow up along the edge of the decomposing wood. It's quiet here, and I feel myself relax. Darren's mellow too. We're pretty far from the camp below—half a mile or so. Maybe a couple of miles from the ranch. I can't hear anything but the aspen leaves whispering in the breeze. That's why they call them "trembling aspens"—because they'll shiver in the slightest wind. It's a sound I love.

I dismount and loosen off Whiskey's saddle. I tie her to a tree so her head can reach the sweet grasses around the base. I tie Springsteen the same way. I unbuckle my saddlebag and grab my water bottle.

"Come on," I say. I'm excited to show Darren around. He seems just as stoked as I am to check out this creepy place.

I show him the mossy old cabin and its built-in wooden bed. The mattress is gone now. Who lived here? What was his life like? The table's still there, next to the four-pane window. Did I just imagine it, or did there used to be old cans and utensils too? I show Darren the rusted-out car beside the cabin. It's a two-door, smaller than I had remembered.

"How'd he get the car up here, I wonder," Darren says.

I glance behind us to where the path we took meets up with another one. "Look there," I say, pointing. "You can see where the road used to lie. Right across the side of the mountain." I look back to the car, imagining the people it once carried. "I wonder why they didn't just build their house in the valley below.

Why would they bother to set this all up on the side of a mountain?"

"They?" asks Darren. He's standing close to me now. Really close. He smells good. Like soap and sunshine. "I thought this was just one crazy mountain man's place," he says.

"Well, maybe," I say. "But I think it *was* a 'they.' Because look at this." I put my hand on his elbow and pull him farther down the narrow trail to where a rusted-out baby carriage rests on its side in the grass. A chill creeps up my back as I look at it. I wonder what happened to that baby.

I shiver. Darren puts his arm around my shoulders. My heart does a giddy little double-skip and I blush a bit, but I don't move under the weight of his arm. I like that he wants to touch me. I want to touch him too, but I don't. Instead I just smile. He smiles back and gives my shoulders a little squeeze.

"Let me show you one more thing," I say. I turn and lead him toward the old well.

The well is covered—at least it used to be. I mean, I sure as hell hope it still is. The grass is pretty long around here. It could easily conceal a well opening. I don't remember exactly where it was, but I seem to recall it was a bit uphill. Just through these bushes. Wasn't it?

I'm bent over and rustling through the greenery, trying to part the thick undergrowth with my hands. There it is. It's still got its cover. I push the grass to the side, exposing a mossy wooden disc.

I don't hear Darren come up behind me. But I feel him. Without warning, he grabs my hips and presses his pelvis against me. Against my butt.

Being this close to him doesn't feel so nice this time.

"Hey!" I shout. I kind of laugh. But it's one of those uncomfortable laughs. You know the ones. Like when you're not sure what's really going on. "What the hell?" I try to stand up. I don't like this. I want to shake him off.

But Darren's hands grip the sides of my hips, an iron vise. He holds me there. Hard. I can't move away. My laughter dies in my throat.

"Darren!" I shout. "Let me go!" I'm pissed now. My voice cracks. I taste fear. I lunge forward but I can't slip his grasp. He laughs.

My mouth suddenly feels like it's full of cotton. I try to stand, but my hands can't push me up off the ground. He's too strong. I don't want to drop to the ground either. I need my legs under me.

I need to run.

Chapter Six

My heart is smashing against my ribcage. I'm tingling everywhere. In the space of a minute this whole situation just went from feeling pretty good to feeling really wrong.

In front of me, my fingers try to grab something—anything—to pull me away from Darren. But there's nothing

sweetheart. He pulls me close to him. Presses his face against mine. His mouth against my ear. Breathes his terrible air onto my cheek.

"It's okay, Jill," he says. His voice is smooth. "Don't be scared." He lets out a spooky little giggle. His voice drops to a whisper. "I'm not going to hurt you. Not yet. I'm just going to play with you a little bit first."

Chapter Seven

Darren drops my arm. I stagger backward. I watch him stroll a few steps away and sit down on a log at the edge of the clearing. He smiles at me. I suppress a crazy urge to laugh as he punches a piece of gum out of a crinkling blister pack and pops it in his mouth. I guess even bad guys need fresh breath.

The urge to giggle passes quickly. An icy fist grips my heart as I remember where I am. Like I'm in some terrible dream, I watch as Darren lifts his pant leg and slides a gleaming hunting knife out of the holster strapped to his calf. *Sssshiinnnng.*

That's when the tears start to roll.

As soon as the sob bubbles up in my throat, I clamp down on it. I can't let myself cry now. It'll screw up my thinking. I've got to think. I don't want him to hear me either. I don't want him to think he's got me where he wants me. Guys like this, fear turns them on.

I tear my eyes off the knife.

Without warning, I hear the voice of my grade-eight gym teacher, Mrs. Rodney.

"You always have a choice," she says in her trademark calm tone. "You can choose fear. Or you can choose focus.

But you can't have both. You don't have room for both." It's the same thing she said to me before our last gymnastics competition—the one where our team flattened every other school in the province and took home the provincial championship title. "It's one or the other," she's saying. "What's it going to be, Jill?"

Right there I ditch the fear and choose focus instead. It's like they're shirts of a different color. Fear won't get me out of here. Fear will kill me. I slide the fear shirt off and slip into the focus one. I imagine that it's made of a fine chain mail. It has a nice weight to it. My feet grow solid under me.

I've got to get off this mountain.

"Listen, Darren," I say. I scuff my toes on the dirt, ignoring his freaky knife. My voice sounds surprisingly steady. I have to talk my way out of this, somehow. "I'm sorry I got mad back there. You just...caught me off guard. Surprised me. Let's just forget about it. Start over, 'kay?" I shrug. "We've seen the mill. Let's go down the mountain and I'll take you to Broken Bridges. There's some pretty cool stuff to see down there too."

The wranglers travel the Broken Bridges trail at least once every couple of hours. Hikers use it too, lots. It runs along the riverside, in plain view of the water and its constantly shifting audience of rafters and kayakers. Lots of people. People who can help get me out of this insane situation that I've suddenly found myself in.

The knife's blade glints in the sunshine. I can see it at the edge of my vision. He's pulled it out to frighten me. He's watching me, waiting for me to lose my head and wig out. I keep my eyes glued to the ground.

"What do you say?" I ask.

He sighs, almost happily. I listen as the knife slides back into its sheath. I look over to where he's sitting. He stretches out in the morning sun, catlike. He grins. "Nah," he says. "I like it up here." He's in no rush, I can see that. He pats the ground beside him. "Have a seat, Jilly Bean." My heart sinks.

I don't want to go over there. I don't want to sit next to him. Next to that knife. What can I say? I've run out of words. I don't know how to steer this conversation, don't know what to say to a deranged guy who carries a knife and presses himself against virtual strangers. What do I do?

I know there's a cell tower on top of this ridge. I've seen it dozens of times. If I can get to my phone inside my saddlebag, I can call for help. I kick myself for taking it out of my chest pocket this morning—but why wouldn't I have? I always do when I ride. I don't want it to shake itself out when I'm galloping through the forest.

Phoning out is a good plan, but I can't call anyone without first getting to my horse. I look over at Whiskey. She's only a few feet away, but I need a good reason if I'm going to be walking that way instead of toward Darren.

"Okay." I shrug, making sure I sound like I have a choice in the matter. "We can stay for a while. But I gotta re-tie the horses or else they'll tangle in their ropes."

I gesture with my thumb to where Whiskey's rope has slid to the bottom of the tree trunk. She grazes calmly, oblivious to my near-death situation.

I squint up at the sky, shading my eyes against the sun. "And I need my sunscreen. It's hotter than a Texas desert out here." That was a cheesy thing to say, I think. But then, I'm not really thinking straight, am I? It's hard to cough up light banter once you've found out your companion is a raving sociopath.

Darren's obviously not worried that I'm going to bolt, because he nods and waves me toward the horses. But he watches me all the same. I feel his eyes on me as I move—*Slow! Keep it casual, Jill!*—toward Whiskey. Just a few steps. There.

When I reach the horse, an outrageous idea hits me. Her rope, having slipped down the tree trunk, is on the ground now. I could easily untie her without him noticing.

Moving calmly, I step directly on the lead rope. I twist my foot slightly as I pass Whiskey's lowered head. I keep moving, toward her hindquarters, where the saddlebag sits. I catch the other section of rope with my other foot and tug on it. The quick-release knot slides apart on the grass. I blink, stunned that it worked so easily. What if I'd tied her with a bowline this morning instead of a quick-release knot? What then?

But I didn't tie a bowline. Today, for some reason, I didn't tie a bowline. I send the universe a silent message of thanks.

Don't look at the rope on the ground. I yank my eyes up. Reach for the saddlebag. My hands shake as I unbuckle the flap, and I need to stop what I'm doing for a second. I take a deep breath. No fear here.

No. Fear. Here.

I slide my hand into the saddlebag and grab the phone. *Yes.* I flip it open. And this is right about where the plan fails. Now that I've got the phone in my hand, I can't see to dial any numbers unless I take it out of the saddlebag.

Darren saves me the trouble of making a decision about this problem. He must have sensed I was up to something. With the stealth of a cougar he's crept up behind me. His hand snakes out and grabs mine. He pulls my hand—and the phone—out of the saddlebag. He turns me around to face him. I swallow.

"Oops," I say brightly. "That's not my sunscreen, now, is it?"

Darren's eyes glitter as he looks into my face. Cold.

"You weren't thinking of calling for help, now, were you, Jilly Bean?" He speaks softly. "Something that stupid could get you killed, you know."

His voice is calm, but his actions are violent as he wrests the phone out of my hand. He takes a couple of steps backward. His eyes bore into mine. Then he raises his hand above his head and slams the phone down hard, against a rock. *SMASH!*

Again. *SMASH!*

Again. *SMASH!*

The phone splinters into a thousand fragments that catch and reflect the sunlight. My head swims at the scene I'm witnessing. Fear stabs at me again and I push it away. I have to stay calm. I can't give him what he wants.

As he pummels the phone against the rock, time suspends itself. I think about my life in clips, like a PowerPoint slideshow. Mum. Dad. Tyler. School. My friends. Tasha telling me I was crazy to come and work in the country. Hannah telling me I should lie about my age and work with them at the nightclub instead.

"C'mon, Jill-O," she had said. "It's easy money. Guys *love* the shooter girls. You'll make huge tips."

But I had shaken my head. "No thanks," I'd said. "I don't want to be groped on a nightly basis by drunken idiots."

Jeez, Jill. I guess you'd rather be groped by a crazy knife-wielding sociopath instead.

I can't help myself. At this last thought, I break into deep, braying laughter.

Abruptly Darren freezes. His eyes narrow. I stop laughing. He throws the hollow shell of the phone aside. Bends over. Lifts the leg of his jeans. He's going for his knife.

Suddenly the fear returns, sharp and hot. It joins my focus, giving me desperate strength.

Without thinking, I swing my leg back and drive the pointed toe of my boot forward as hard as I can. Into his face. I hear a crunch, followed by a wet sucking sound.

Darren roars in pain. He falls forward, on his knees, the knife temporarily forgotten. Splinters of white teeth drop from his bloodied mouth.

Wow. That was amazing. *I* did that?

Darren looks up at me, surprised, like I've betrayed him. His face is a wet red mess. My stomach heaves.

I turn and grab Whiskey's saddle horn. I swing up as Darren lurches to his feet, one hand clamped against his mouth. My feet just find the stirrups as he grabs for my leg with his other hand.

Frantically I shake him off and pound Whiskey with my heels. She pitches forward. Away from the bleeding, staggering fiend beside us. Darren roars again. He snatches at Whiskey's tail. I hammer on her flanks.

And just like that, we're away. My heart swells up, a balloon filling my entire body with relief. My breath squeaks through the narrow opening in my throat. *We're good, we're good, we're good, we're good.* The sound bite skips in my head, over and over and over.

Then the saddle slips.

Chapter Eight

Not much. Just a bit. And with it, my heart gives a sudden lurch and lands in my stomach. I forgot that I had loosened off Whiskey's saddle. How could I forget?

Well, really. It's not like I could've stood there and tightened up her cinch while Darren-the-wacko was smashing my lifeline to smithereens. There wasn't time.

I feel the saddle slip again, and I yank myself in the other direction. I might be able to keep it straight just by jerking it back into place every time it slips. Darren's outraged shouts follow us as we plunge down the trail. He's fast, for a guy who's just had his face rearranged. Not as fast as the horse. But if I fall off...

The saddle slips again, and a blast of adrenaline rockets through my body. My mind races, flipping through choices like a stack of cards. I could slow to a walk and try to yank the saddle back into place. But Darren might catch up—and the saddle would still be loose, besides. Or I could quickly dismount, tighten the cinch and jump back on before Darren catches me. Right. With these shaking fingers? Or...I could just see how far I can go with a loose cinch. Maybe—

Without warning, the saddle slides clean around Whiskey's barrel, taking me with it. On my way down, I grab for her mane and halter. Small bushes whip my face as I find myself suddenly at ground level. I duck and shut my eyes.

My grabbing arms pull Whiskey's head to the side. Fists full of mane and rope, I heave and scramble up onto her back.

But she's not having any of it. Like any horse, she knows the saddle belongs on her back, not on her belly. Whiskey bucks, trying to get free of the strange sensation. She's scared. I'm scared.

She bucks again. I cling.

She runs faster. Realizing she's still stuck with the saddle, she bucks again, serious this time. She throws her head down at the same moment that her rear comes up. I can't hang on. With a heavy thump, Whiskey's butt knocks me clean off her back, like a catapult. I cartwheel into space.

I hit the ground with a *whump* and lie there, gasping for air. I can't get any. Someone's emptied out my lungs and tied off my throat. I hear Whiskey's hoofbeats as she thunders off down the path.

Unable to breathe, I swirl into darkness.

Chapter Nine

My head hurrrrrrrrrts. Augh. *Aaugggh.*

I open my eyes slowly. I come to, surrounded by green. I'm looking up into the dark forest canopy. With a slow, dreadful precision, the morning's events slide into place in my memory. I stifle a moan as everything comes back into focus. I close my eyes again. If Darren is still around, I don't want to know. Not just yet.

My head is pounding. I must still be alive.

I crack my eyelids a bit, surveying the scene. I'm lying in the dirt, on my back, with my legs splayed out in front of me. Blood smears the toe of my right boot. It mixes with the dried-up horse-shit, and I almost smile. I wonder how *that* tasted? My jeans are streaked with dirt. My chaps are off, piled in a heap beside Darren, who's sitting on a rock ten feet away. I feel a wash of terror.

The knife is out again, and Darren is cleaning his fingernails with the tip of the blade. He's humming, absorbed in his sick grooming ritual. As I watch, a tiny rivulet of red trickles from underneath one nail. I suppress a shudder of revulsion.

Focus. Not fear.

I tear my eyes away from the bleeding mess and shift my attention to the noises around us. I strain my ears, but all I can hear are the leaves of the aspen trees around us whispering in the breeze.

I look around without moving my head. We're up high, on an outcropping. I'm lying in a clearing with my back up against a small cliff of dirt. I'm sore all over after being pitched off Whiskey's back. I curl my toes inside my boots. No pain. I can still feel my legs. Good.

Slowly I flex the muscles in my arms. Where are my fingers? I can't feel them. Concentrating, I will them to move. Ah. There they are, somewhere above my head. They're tingling a bit. I try to move my hands apart, but I can't. I think my wrists have been tied.

My shoulder throbs where Darren twisted it earlier. I look back at him, making sure he's still intent upon his macabre grooming. Then I steal a quick peek up above me.

My heart sinks. He's tied me up. My hands are knotted together and then tied to an exposed tree root in the crumbling cliff face. The root is old and gnarled, covered in green lichen. I can't see past it to the ledge above, so I can't tell how big the tree is. Damn.

But in looking around, I've placed myself. We're on the west ridge. There's an aspen grove below us—an army of white trunks that march into the woods as far as the eye can see. There's only one grove like it anywhere near the ranch.

I must have made it pretty far on Whiskey before I fell off. Either that or Darren dragged me here. Surveying the state of my jeans, I figure he probably dragged me.

But now he's the stupid one. Because the river runs right beside the aspen grove below us. And right beside the river runs the main trail. Darren won't know this. He can't hear the river over the constant *sssshhh*ing of the aspens. It's a good thing he stopped where he did. If he hadn't been halted by the steep embankment, he'd have kept dragging me until he stumbled on the river. Then he'd have turned around and taken me right back into the bushes. And I'd be another statistic.

But I'm not a statistic yet. And I don't plan to be either.

I look up at the blue sky. Around at the shadows. I figure we've been gone a couple of hours. If the eleven o'clock ride went out on the river path, like the one-hour trips almost always do, there's bound to be a whole string of people passing below me in the next while. My heart beats faster at the thought of being rescued.

I look at Darren. He stares back. He knows I'm awake now.

My hope drains fast. I might not have very long.

"Well, well," he drawls. A misshapen grin twists his ruined face, and my gut knots with a sudden rush of adrenaline. "Seems like Jilly Bean's gotten herself into a whole lot of trouble," he says. Except, without his teeth, it comes out: *Theemth like Zilly beanth gotten herthelf into a whole lot of twouble.* I bite my lips against a sudden smile.

"You better not try anything thtoopid again," he lisps. With a demented leer, Darren brings the knife up into full view.

My urge to smile vaporizes. He turns the knife this way and that. I can't take my eyes off the enormous shiny blade.

I swallow, and my dry throat clicks. I cough.

He looks at me again. He stands slowly, gripping the knife loosely in his hand. Casual, like he's not just about to stab another human being to death. He doesn't take his eyes off me.

Before I even decide I'm going to do it, I swing my boots ferociously upward, at the hand holding the knife. *Thock!*

Perfect contact. The knife flies out of his hand—and right into the mound of dirt beside me.

No. NO! I almost scream in frustration. I kicked it the wrong way. If I'd kicked it the other way, it would've sailed off the edge of our little cliff and down into the trees, never to be found. What was I thinking? What was I *thinking*?

Surprised, Darren looks at his empty hand. He looks at the knife.

I'm not about to wait for him to pick it up. I flail my feet toward his crotch, connecting squarely with a sickening thump. He grunts and folds forward. I keep kicking, like a toddler having a tantrum on the supermarket floor.

Doubled over, he holds his crotch with one hand and shields himself from my relentless kicking with the other. I almost feel sorry for him. I'm putting up a pretty good fight. Not such an easy victim.

This last thought sobers me. I might be winning the battle, but I'm far from winning the war. I'm still stuck with a fruitcake rapist with a knife who's going to recover soon from the testicular trauma I've inflicted on him. And I'm still tied to a tree in the middle of the forest, where no one can see me or hear me.

Hear me! Why has it taken me so long to think of screaming? Feet still pinwheeling, I gather up a huge gawp of breath and start to holler.

Chapter Ten

I gotta hand it to this guy. Even through his pain, he can move fast. No sooner does the first sound issue from my lungs than the jerk is sitting on my chest, pressing a cloth into my open mouth. He shoves it in so far I think I'm going to suffocate. I try to push it forward with my tongue. Reaching into his pocket, he whips out a length of beige nylon and ties it around the back of my head. He knots it severely across my cheek. Pantyhose? Whose were *these?* My scalp crawls.

I'm sickened by the idea that he had this all planned. While I was telling him my life story, this nut was planning how he'd take me into the woods and rape and kill me. Was he thinking it through, step by step, as he watched me round up the horses this morning? Why did he pick me? Why couldn't Carrie and Laura have been there to see me leave this morning? Why didn't I go back and double-check his registration?

Unanswerable questions swirl inside my mind. I close my eyes, willing myself not to vomit. If I puke now, I'll choke on it and die.

I feel the tears welling up in my throat again, and I force them away. I have to keep thinking, keep moving. Keep trying to get out of this unbelievable mess.

"Stupid whore," Darren slurs, pulling my legs together and sitting on my thighs. *Thtoopid.* Now I can't move at all. He reaches forward and plucks the knife up off the dirt from where it fell.

I can't stop myself this time. I sob. Tears squeeze out of the corners of my eyes.

Like a little kid who's just spied his Christmas stocking, Darren looks at me, delighted. A surprised smile crinkles his eyes. He blinks, absently running his thumb along the knife's edge. New tears fall as I watch the sharp blade neatly disappear into the fleshy pad of his thumb. Droplets of red blood rise to the surface, then ooze toward his wrist.

He puts his thumb in his mouth and sucks it. I taste bile in my throat. Sucking his bloodied thumb, he looks down at me and moans.

He's a lunatic.

As suddenly as it came on, my despair evaporates. Disgust and fury take its place. Through the gag I growl my revulsion. I wave my hands at him. He looks up at them, and I pop my fists forward, jabbing my middle fingers in the air. His smile shrinks slowly and his eyes narrow as they meet mine. Maybe I've done the wrong thing, but this loser doesn't get me without all the fight I can give.

Suddenly Darren lunges at me, shoving his face into mine. His pupils are huge and black, like something dead.

"I'm gonna kill you slow, Jilly," he whispers. His tongue snakes out of his torn-up mouth and eases its way along my face. I gag.

He sits up, breathing heavily, and looks at me for a moment. Then he smiles, sliding the knife under one of the buttons on my shirt.

Ping. The button pops into the air, almost comical.

Ping. Another one.

Ping.

My head swims. Darkness claws at the edge of my thoughts. How long until they find my body? What if he drags me deep into the bushes? Panic threatens to choke me, and I shove it down. It bounces back, like a beach ball popping to the surface of a lake.

What's he going to do with the knife?

Darren hears my thoughts and opens his bloody grin into my face. "They're gonna find you in a million" *ping* "little" *ping* "pieces."

Ping. The last button pops off. I squeeze my eyes shut, willing myself into a happy place. Sunshine, our kitchen, beaches, a Starbucks vanilla latte.

I open my eyes, forcing myself back into the scene. Darren's forehead drips sweat. He's panting with the effort of sawing off my clothes. Blood smears his handsome features. His mouth is a ragged, torn mess of bleeding gums and broken teeth.

I don't want to die here. Anger washes over me at my situation. At my helplessness.

Screw this, I think. With a super-adrenalized heave, I pull downward with both arms. "*RRRAAAAAAARRGGGHH!*" I roar through my gag like a cornered animal.

The root I'm tied to doesn't budge.

But the tree does.

With a groan, the old tree shifts in the parched soil that's weathered away from underneath it.

Startled, Darren looks up. That's when I yank again. With a loud crunch, the tree gives way. It sails through the air, its muddy roots neatly clearing my body. I can see now that it's a huge old stump. Time suspends itself for a moment. I gaze in awe as the stump floats through the airspace above me. It must weigh more than I do.

It smashes Darren across the chest, knocking him backward into the dirt and jerking me into a sitting position. I blink, surprised to find myself in a different situation so quickly.

Wrangler 1: Psycho 0.

From beneath the wooden mass, Darren moans. He's still conscious.

Crap. His groaning clears my head. Darren might be down, but I'm still tied to a hundred-pound stump. There will be no running away until I get free of it.

Chapter Eleven

Frenzied, I kick at the root to which my hands are tied. It breaks on the third blow, and I scramble to my feet.

I pelt away through the shrubby undergrowth, my feet guiding me toward one of the narrow deer trails that follow the ridge. I'm certain it will take me down to the river. That's where all animal paths lead.

My whole body feels supercharged, like I'm made of electricity. My hands are still tied, but I tuck them up against my chest. I throw my elbows out for balance. I jump, smooth and strong, over fallen logs, ducking and dodging the hanging branches. This is definitely what it feels like to be a deer. I'm almost enjoying myself, except for the fact that there's a crazed murderer pinned under a tree stump behind me.

Ah, but I should know better. He's not just any crazed murderer. This is Darren Parker we're speaking of. The insane, inescapable, undefeatable Darren Parker. I snort, briefly envisioning him chasing me through the forest in a pink bunny outfit, beating on a big Energizer drum.

So when I hear his footsteps behind me on the path, I'm hardly surprised. He just loves the chase, this guy. And I just can't get him to give up on it, no matter

how many times I try. I realize that it's
probably his favorite part.

But the last thing I want is to be
caught again. Because I know there
won't be any third chances. If he
catches me this time, he'll finish me off
wherever I fall.

I hear his breathing now, heavy and
rhythmic. He's maybe twenty feet back.

My brain sweeps away all the
hysterical chatter, and I calmly size up
the situation. On one side of me, the
pine forest sweeps up the mountainside, dark and tightly packed. Straight
ahead, the deer path runs as far as I can
see along the grassy ridge. To my left,
the embankment plunges one hundred
feet to the aspen canopy below.

I can't climb through the forest. He's
stronger and faster, and he'll catch me.

I can't keep running. My chest is
about to burst. I can't breathe through

this gag. And I can't possibly outrun him with my arms tied.

But I'm not ready to die.

At least, not on his terms.

I veer sharply to the left. Over the cliff. Into space.

Chapter Twelve

I expected to die. I'm almost tired of not dying, tired of having to keep going in this ridiculous game of cat and mouse. I am a tired mouse now, and I want to quit playing.

But I can't. Not while I've still got juice in me. Not while there's a possibility that that busted-up freakjob is still out there, looking for me.

The way I figure it, Darren wouldn't have dared to follow me off the cliff. It's just way too high to survive the fall. He—like me—would have had no idea about the rotting log at the bottom. Or the dozens of soft fir branches that come in pretty handy for breaking a fall.

I look around me. Crazy. I'm on all fours, buried up to my elbows in soft, damp tree crumbs. My neck aches from whiplash, and I've got tiny red chunks of Douglas fir in my nostrils, but somehow I'm still alive.

I push up with my hands and try to stand in the pile of decaying wood. But it's too thick and soft, and I fall over with a *flump*. I lie there for a moment, suddenly ecstatic. I'm alive! What are the chances?

But I still have to get out of here. I've got to get to safety. I've got to find people. Before that creep finds *me*.

The idea of getting caught galvanizes me. I roll down from the rotting heap and stand on shaky legs. I slide my thumbs under the nylon that's tied around my face. I pull. The band tightens behind my head. With a squeaking sound, the thin band of synthetic fabric stretches. I've managed to loosen it off a bit. I work it over my face and throw it into the bushes. I push the gag out of my mouth with my dry tongue. Fresh air, cool and moist, rushes into my body. It feels like I'm drinking a cloud.

I wish I could get this rope off my hands! I look around for something sharp—a rock. But there's nothing around except grass, trees and wildflowers. I wonder briefly how much farther the ridge path continues before it descends down to the level of the river. How long until Darren reaches the trail junction? How long will it take him to double back on the river path and find me?

A small animal rustles in the leaves near my feet, and I jump. Panic suddenly grips me, and I bolt. I follow the gradual downhill slope, toward the river. I can see blue-green water sparkling in the sunlight. I've got to get to the main trail.

I pound through the bushes, down, down, down. When my feet hit the hardpack of the river path, I'm flooded with relief. I nearly fall to the ground with gratitude.

I look up and down the path. No sign of anyone. I look upstream as far as I can see. There's no one on the river either.

It's funny: I hadn't considered that there wouldn't be anyone around. I hadn't thought any farther than reaching the river path. In my confused terror, I had just assumed that someone would be standing there, waiting for me with a blanket and a cup of hot coffee. But no one's waiting here for me. I'm still alone. Being chased by a sinister, blood-streaked madman.

I hear him before I can see him. Oh. My. God. This will never end. This is my own private hell that I've been thrown into. Perhaps it's payback for teasing my friend Jennifer about shaving her legs in fifth grade. Maybe it's karmic retaliation for eating the last of Brenda's chocolate-covered digestive cookies when she fell asleep on the ski bus. Or maybe it's penance for publishing pictures of naked people in my high-school newspaper.

I giggle then, high and thin and on the edge of sanity.

In the distance, Darren appears on the path. He's shouting, but his missing teeth distort the words. I can't make out what he's saying. Not that it matters. He's an enraged hornet who can't get his victim to stand still long enough to sting.

I want to stay on the path, but there's no way I can outrun him.

The river's green waters churn at my feet. It's deep and it's fast and I don't have a life jacket and my hands are tied together and there's a shitty set of rapids ahead that will drown me, but it's the only place I can think of to get away from this psycho.

I close my eyes briefly. A deep sigh tears itself from the bottom of my soul and issues from my cracked and bleeding lips.

Eyes still closed, I jump.

Chapter Thirteen

The frigid water of the glacier-fed river shocks me back into myself. When my lungs recover, I take a big gulp of air for flotation and turn over onto my back.

I won't think about the rapids ahead. Won't think about the fact that I nearly died when I swam through them two years ago during river-guide training.

They made us jump off the side and go through what the guides call Hell's Gorge: a sphincter-clenching stretch of whirlpools and washing machines and standing waves. That was *with* a wet suit, *with* a life jacket and *with* free hands. It was terrifying.

I can see Darren running along the shore. He's doing a creepy little skipping dance as he follows me along. The river's current is fast, but he's faster on the ground. I wonder if he'll jump in to catch me. God, I hope not. He probably won't. He told me he's not a great swimmer.

Wait. Maybe that would be a good thing then.

Jump! I think. *Jump, you freak!* He doesn't.

I scan the bank but see no sign of the eleven o'clock ride. *Where are they?* Suddenly my earlier optimism dissolves. Darren might not be coming out here into the water to get me, but unless someone stops him on the path, he'll be waiting for me when I finally wash up on the shore, gasping and hypothermic.

Unless I swim to the other side, I realize. The First Nations reserve is on that side. Surely I could drag myself out over there and walk to someone's house and ask to use the phone.

I glance at the bank again. He's still there, hopping along. His hands are up beside his face, and he's dancing around like he's in the circus ring. How can there be room for so much craziness in just one brain?

As I watch, he stops for a moment to take out his knife. Then he resumes his twisted dance, waving the knife in the air. His laughter reaches my ears. He's loving this. He knows he's going to win. I shudder, only partly from the freezing water.

No.

He's *not* going to win.

Still on my back, I angle myself toward the other shore and start to kick.

The water is fast. I fight the instinctive urge to put my feet down on the bottom. We watched a Red Cross video in outdoor education class last year that showed what happens when you try to stand up in a fast-flowing river. They showed a bird's-eye view of a real guy whose foot got caught between two rocks on the riverbed. He got stuck. And the water just…folded him over and held him there. Against the bottom. I was so messed up by watching the accident that I don't remember whether they were able to save him. I just know that the image burned itself onto my brain.

I raise my head briefly to see how much farther I have to go before I reach the other shore. My heart leaps into my throat. A huge sweeper lies dead ahead. The fallen tree leans out over the water. Its roots are still bound by the bank, but its branches and trunk trail on the river's surface. It's a hundred feet away yet, but I know I won't be able to change my line quickly enough to avoid it. I scan the length of the sweeper frantically, looking for a place that's free of branches. Maybe I'll be able to slip through without getting caught.

Because if I'm caught, I'm done. The branches will tangle in my clothes and hair, and they'll hold me in the tree until I drown or freeze to death.

But maybe it wouldn't be so bad to get caught in the sweeper, I reflect. Because without my hands, I'm going to drown in the rapids ahead.

I don't have a choice in the matter anyway. The river's current swirls me downstream, right toward the dying tree. Time's up. I close my eyes as the water slides me in, under the big trunk. At the last moment it occurs to me that I could dive down, deep under the water's surface, in hopes of avoiding the branches.

But it's too late. The sweeper snags me and I stop moving. It holds me in its grip. The water pushes furiously against me, rushing in a wave around my head as it tries to drag me along downstream.

I open my eyes. My face is above water. I can still breathe. That's good. That's amazing, actually. I'm on the downstream side of the sweeper's trunk, floating on my back. The river's force stretches my body out, filling my boots and pulling my feet downstream. My shoulder screams that it's being pulled apart. I kick off my boots. Too much weight.

One boot comes up to float near the surface, half submerged. I watch as it fills with water and sinks out of sight. I glance over at the shore, but I don't see Darren. My heart lurches. Where is he? If I can't see him, where is he?

I'm on the downstream side of the sweeper, nearly free of it. But I'm caught by the rope around my wrists. A stout branch has jabbed itself right in between my hands, under the rope. It impales my wrists against the tree. The branch is on the upstream side of the trunk, and I'm on the downstream side. There's no way I can drag myself upstream enough to bend my elbows and pull my hands off the peg. Not even the Incredible Hulk could do it. The river's pulling at me with about three hundred pounds of pressure. I'm stuck.

Bloodied, battered and completely exhausted, the utter futility of my situation sinks in. My teeth start chattering. I try to stop them. I've experienced the onset of hypothermia before. I know the chattering will feed my panic and will make it hard for me to think.

Think.

I feel around with my thumbs. Can I

hook one under the rope? I twist my hands around in their prison, straining my muscles to feel for a place where I can ease my thumb under. The water has loosened the rope a bit. I'm able to pull one of the loops toward my thumb. I slide my thumb under—*yes!* I wedge my palm after it.

Lubricated by the rushing water, the loop slides over my hand. I keep poking my thumbs around, looking for the next loop to slip off. Another loop slides free. I feel the rope loosen around both my wrists.

My heart skips out a hopeful beat, but I force my attention back to what I'm doing. I wiggle both hands like an awkwardly jointed butterfly. *Flap. Flap.* The rope slithers away from my hands.

I leave it there, twined around the branch.

The river swings me downstream.

Toward Hell's Gorge.

Chapter Fourteen

I've got about two minutes before the rapids start. Plenty of time to get out. I look ahead to make sure there aren't any other sweepers waiting to grab me in their woody embrace. Nope, the water ahead is clear. I angle toward the near shore, toward the reserve, kicking my freezing legs. I paddle with arms that feel like they're made of lead.

I'm pretty close to the edge now.

Suddenly I spot the hole in my plan. The bank isn't grassy or sandy. It's not even gravelly. It's just a wall of rock. And it's, like, twenty-five feet high.

Being the start of a gorge and all.

I don't even allow myself a second of whining at this newest awful development in my day. I'm cold, and I'm growing stupid as my awareness slowly dwindles to a pinprick centered on surviving this crappy mess. I've got to save my mental energy for getting me through the rapids. I can't climb out on this side. And that stupid freak stabber guy is somewhere on the other side. I have no choice.

I have to swim them.

I flip onto my stomach and point my head downstream. I force my arms to paddle as the roar of the approaching rapids gets louder. If I'm going to avoid getting sucked under, I've got to be going either faster than the water, or slower. Without a boat and paddle, there's no way I can control my speed enough to slow down. But I can swim faster than the current.

So I do. I pinwheel my leaden arms and kick hard, trying to keep my head above the surface so I can see dangerous rocks. I've piloted plenty of rafts through this canyon before. But things look different from up high, on top of the water's surface. Down here, things happen fast, and it's hard to see through all the splashing white water. I'm not sure where everything is, but I remember the major features.

The roar becomes deafening. Then suddenly there's a drop.

I'm in. The thunder of pounding water fills my head. I gulp mouthful upon mouthful of icy water as I hurtle my way through the churning mass of waves. Up, down, under.

My right ankle glances against a submerged rock. I suck in a freezing gulp. My left knee smashes squarely into another rock. I scream and choke. I paddle harder, lifting my head high to see what's in front of me.

I crest a large standing wave and stare around, planning my line. I'm a quarter of the way through, but the worst is still ahead. I'm pretty sure my kneecap is broken. I kick anyway.

This is such. A bad. Day. My eyes catch a glimpse of a red shirt on the shore and I feel a wave of relief.

Relief? That's kind of twisted.

Yeah, I guess it is twisted. You know things are messed up when you're relieved to see the crazy nutcase who's out to knife you to death.

But if I can see him, at least I know where he is. Better over there than creeping up on me in the water. He's got a huge branch, and he's dragging it along the trail behind him. What the hell is he up to now?

I slip into the trough of one wave and kick up to the top of the next one. I'm in the center channel now, away from most of the rocks, but the most deadly rapid still lies ahead.

The river twists and turns as it slides through the canyon in a fast-moving S-curve. I skid around a corner and experience a momentary thrill. A finger of piled rocks juts out from the shore, almost to the center of the river. I could climb out before hitting the weir!

But as soon as the thought occurs to me I realize it's impossible. I'd be climbing right into a death sentence. Because somewhere over there, Darren is waiting for me. With a knife. And now a big branch.

He's waiting for me to give up. Waiting for me to swim, broken and freezing, to the shore.

I look ahead. Scratch that last bit. He's not waiting for me to come to him. He's going to *catch* me. And he's got himself a big-ass fishin' pole to do the job.

I watch in horror as Darren strolls to the end of the pile of rocks. He's got the big branch slung over his shoulder. As I watch, he lifts the branch and then lowers it over the water. He's planning to hook me with it and drag me to shore.

And I'm helpless to stop him.

The current sweeps me past the outcropping. He leans out from the rocks, a bleeding monster. He jabs the branch at me, snagging my shirt. I reach back, fumbling. Trying to free my collar from the branch's woody tip. I can't. My fingers are too cold. They won't bend far enough. I scream in frustration and fear.

The water swings me, held fast by the branch, around the point of rock toward the eddy below. If I cross into the slow-moving water of the eddy, Darren will be able to fish me out easily. And kill me. Unless I can somehow stop myself from being pulled to shore.

Either way, I'll probably die. But I'd rather die in the rapids downstream, thanks. And then a thought hits me. It's a perfect thought, round and bright and easy for my tired mind to grasp. It's scary as hell, but it's the only way I can see an end to this madness.

Without a moment's hesitation, I reach behind me with both arms. I clamp my freezing hands around the branch. I pull hard. With a shout, Darren lets go of the branch—but it's too late. Yanked sharply off his feet, he lands with a splash in the water behind me. My frozen cheeks stretch into a grin.

Really, it's a pity that he's not much of a swimmer.

Because I'm going to introduce this clown to my treacherous little friend.

The Widowmaker.

Chapter Fifteen

Now that Darren's in the river with me, I'm not taking any chances. I want to get as far away from him as possible. I duck my head and pull harder, trying to swim as fast as I can. I kick and thrash my way through the standing waves, closer to the center of the channel. That's where a narrow green tongue of water pours clean over the ledge and doesn't curl back on itself like the rest of the Widowmaker does. If I can ride the green tongue, I might make it out alive.

From below, something grabs at my foot. I scream wildly, kicking out with both feet. I pinwheel my arms and turn myself around, drawing my legs up under me. But it's nothing. Just my mind playing tricks. The thunderous roar of the Widowmaker edges closer now.

Not far behind me, Darren splashes angrily around in the rapids. His mangled face bobs up and down with the current. I wish I could swim away and never see it again.

I realize my fight against the imaginary foot-grabber has taken me off course. I'm not lined up properly to catch the green tongue. Things are moving very quickly now.

Instead of slipping through the safe channel, I slide over a huge ledge and into the foamy hole below. I feel it rather than see it, and dread seizes my heart.

This wasn't supposed to happen.

For a moment I forget about Darren and his knife and his broken face and his desire to cut me apart. As soon as I realize what's happening, I begin to kick and thrash with my legs and arms. I need to move faster than the water.

I can't get sucked into the hole.

But I can't break away. Panic fills me as the wash pulls me down into the frothy white trap.

"NO! Nooooooooo!" My voice sounds like it's a thousand light-years away. Thin and muffled around the edges. My eyes bug as I claw at the water ahead of me. "NO!" I kick hysterically, so much that my hips threaten to fly out of their sockets. I scream every swear I can think of, cursing the weir and its single-minded mission to swallow me into its huge hydraulic tumbler. I've seen entire canoes go under this kind of rapid. If I go in, I won't come out until the river dries up or until the Widowmaker spits me out whenever it damn well pleases. It could be hours. It could be weeks. I'll just roll around under the wave with all the other flotsam that it's trapped over the years. Logs. Life jackets. Bits of boats.

Darren.

I sob at this last thought, clawing harder.

And then, inexplicably, I pop free. Gasping and pinwheeling, I shoot away from the deadly rapid and hurtle downstream, still stuck in my churning white-water nightmare. I piston around and stare, wild-eyed, behind me.

I turn just in time to see something red plunge over the ledge.

Exhausted and afraid to believe my eyes, I stop paddling. I stare, unwilling to take my eyes off the Widowmaker for fear that Darren will pop back up and lunge toward me. But he doesn't. I watch and wait, but he doesn't.

He doesn't.

The river widens and its current slows as the rapids edge out of sight.

My fight against the river has warmed my body, but I'm completely wrung out. I put my head back and drift for a while, listening to the roar of the water as it smashes its way through Hell's Gorge. Amazingly, I seem to be just as unkillable as Mr. Killer himself.

Except he's been killed now.

The Widowmaker took care of that.

When I can't hear the thunder of the rapids anymore, I lift my head and look around. I scan the riverbank for some sign of horses or hikers, but I see none. I guess there wasn't an eleven o'clock ride after all. Or maybe Carrie and Laura are still asleep and the guests are just hanging around the corral, waiting for the wranglers to show up and start their day. Jeez. To think I was so stressed out about having to round up a piddly bunch of horses on my own this morning! It suddenly strikes me as funny, and I laugh.

When I catch sight of a couple of rafts around a bend in the river ahead, I laugh at that too. There are just two, big and blue and full of helmet-clad people squirting water guns at each other in the July sunshine. They're coming onshore so they can enjoy lunch beside the river. Their voices drift toward me on the mellow breeze.

Calmly, as though I haven't just been chased through the woods by a foaming-at-the-mouth madman, as though I haven't just escaped being murdered and chopped into a billion tiny pieces, as though I haven't just gone to hell and back in the freezing waters of the Sawtooth River, I call to them.

"Hey! Hi!"

The group turns toward me. Blue suits and yellow helmets, like some sort of rubberized army. They scan the water, searching to pinpoint the source of my voice, so unexpected.

"Hi!" I say again. I paddle toward them. They stare. I can't figure out what else to say. I can't think of how to start this conversation, how to tell them what I've just been through.

Seeing that I have no life jacket, several men have waded quickly out into the water. I smile at their chivalry, their instinctive desire to keep me safe from the treachery of the cold water.

If only they knew.

One of them reaches out to me with the butt of his paddle. I grab it with my frozen hands and drift in to the shore, comforted by its smooth plastic shaft. I must look pretty rough, because no one scolds me for being out in the river without a life jacket.

"You're okay now," says one middle-aged guy who could be my own dad. He's watching my face carefully. His voice is soothing. "You're here. We've got you. You're okay." He helps me out of the water, helps me limp up onto the grass where the paddlers were planning to have their lunch.

"Jeez, you're a mess," says another. "Why are you out in this river by yourself? Where's your boat?"

They look around at each other, out at the water. Everyone's talking at once, excited and worried and wanting to help. My teeth chatter. I try to smile but I think it ends up being more of a frozen sneer.

A woman brings a blanket and puts it around my shoulders. "Honey, tell us what happened to you," she says. Her warm voice starts my body shivering.

I chatter and shiver and shake my head, unable to speak. She draws me closer.

Another paddler rubs my back. One of the guides sets about examining my knee through my torn jeans. Another pours me a cup of hot chocolate from a thermos.

I lean against the blanket lady and shake.

"Jill!" A familiar voice cuts through the group's murmuring. I look behind me, toward the path. James is sitting astride his horse, looking both arrogant and worried at the same time. "What the hell? Are you okay? Your horse came running back to the barn with her saddle spun. What's going on?"

Before I can answer him—or swear at him or tell him I quit or laugh at the absurdity of all this help suddenly appearing just moments after I could have really used it—a shout goes up from another of the guides.

"Hey, you guys!"

He's calling from farther up the shore. Our heads all swivel to look.

He's walking quickly down the beach toward the group, holding up something brown for everyone to see. He's young, maybe my age. "Look what washed up just below Hell's Gorge. Is this freaky or what?"

In his hand he holds a leather case. In his other hand a gleaming knife. He brings it over so everyone can have a good look.

Everyone except me. I don't look at the knife. Why would I? I've seen it enough. I hug the blanket closer.

"Honey," says the woman who's holding me. She holds my shoulders, her soft brown eyes looking steadily into mine. She kind of looks like my mum. "Why don't you just start at the beginning?"

Do I have enough words for this? Will I ever?

I take a deep breath and begin to talk.

Alex Van Tol is a freelance writer in Victoria, British Columbia. *Knifepoint* is her first novel. Visit her in the electronic ether at alexvantol.com.

orca soundings

978-1-55469-296-5 $9.95 pb
978-1-55469-297-2 $16.95 lib

BRENDAN, CAPTAIN OF THE BASKETBALL
team, has it all—good friends, a beautiful
girlfriend and a loving family—until he is
diagnosed with leukemia. Terrified and convinced
that no one understands what he is going through,
Brendan faces chemotherapy alone, until he
meets Lark. She is also in treatment, although her
condition is much worse, and yet she remains
positive and hopeful. Brendan is torn between
feeling sorry for himself and the love for life that
Lark brings to even the simplest thing. Through
Lark, he discovers the strength to go on, to fight
for survival and to love.

orca soundings

DIANE TULLSON

SEA CHANGE

978-1-55469-332-0 $9.95 pb
978-1-55469-333-7 $16.95 lib

LUCAS AND HIS FATHER ARE NOT CLOSE.

In fact they hardly see each other, which is just fine
with Lucas. When he travels to the remote fishing
lodge his father manages, Lucas is left once
again, this time with a lodge worker, a girl named
Sumi. She makes it pretty clear that Lucas is on
his own. But she does take him fishing and seems
to be warming up to him. Then, in a horrible
sequence of misjudgments, Sumi is shot in the
foot. With no radio and no phone, Lucas and
Sumi are truly alone. Fog rolls over the islands
and it's up to Lucas to get Sumi to medical help,
a day's journey by boat up the inlet.

orca soundings

978-1-55469-364-1 $9.95 pb
978-1-55469-365-8 $16.95 lib

WHEN DANIEL ENTERS A CONVENIENCE

store on a secret mission, he doesn't expect to run into anyone he knows. That would ruin everything. And when Rosie enters the same store to see what her father wants, she's hoping to make a quick getaway with her waiting boyfriend.

All Daniel and Rosie want is to get in and out without any trouble. Neither expects what happens next. A masked man enters the store.

"This is a stickup," he announces. He has a gun and isn't afraid to use it. When he's ready to leave, he decides to take Rosie hostage.

And then things get complicated...

Titles in the Series

orca soundings

orca soundings

For more information on all the books
in the Orca Soundings series, please visit
www.orcabook.com.